Xavier and the Letter **X**

Alphabet Friends

by Cynthia Klingel and Robert B. Noyed

The
**Child's
World**®

Published in the United States of America
by The Child's World®
P.O. Box 326
Chanhassen, MN 55317-0326
800-599-READ
www.childsworld.com

The Child's World®: Mary Berendes, Publishing Director

Editorial Directions, Inc.: E. Russell Primm, Editorial
Director; Emily Dolbear, Line Editor; Ruth Martin,
Editorial Assistant; Linda S. Koutris, Photo Researcher
and Selector

Photographs ©: Ryan McVay/Photodisc/Getty Images:
Cover & 9, 14; George Disario/Corbis: 10; Corbis: 13,
17, 18; Photodisc/Getty Images: 21.

Library of Congress Cataloging-in-Publication Data
Klingel, Cynthia Fitterer.
  Xavier and the letter X / by Cynthia Klingel and
Robert B. Noyed.
    p. cm. — (Alphabet readers)
Summary: A simple story about a surprise in a box
introduces the letter "x".
  ISBN 1-59296-114-2 (Library Bound : alk. paper)
  [1. Boxes—Fiction. 2. Alphabet.] I. Noyed, Robert B., ill.
II. Title. III. Series.
  PZ7.K6798Xa 2003
  [E]—dc21   2003006612

Note to parents and educators:
The first skill children acquire before becoming successful readers is individual letter recognition. The Alphabet Friends series has been created with the needs of young learners in mind. Each engaging book begins by showing the difference between the capital letter and the lowercase letter. In each of the books on the vowels and the consonants c and g, children are introduced to the different sounds that the letter can make. Finally, children see that the letters can be found at the beginning of a word, in the middle of a word, and in most cases, at the end of a word.

Following the introduction, children meet their Alphabet Friends. The friend in each story encounters many words that include the featured letter of that book. Each noun that begins with the title letter is highlighted in red with the initial letter of the word in bold. Above the word is a rebus drawing that establishes a strong picture cue.

At the end of each book, we have included three words lists. Can your young learners find all the words in each book with the title letter in them?

Let's learn about the letter **X.**

The letter **X** can look like this: **X.**

The letter **X** can also look like this: **x.**

The letter **x** can be at the

beginning of a word, like X ray.

X ray

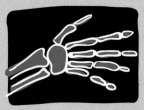

The letter **x** can be in the

middle of a word, like taxicab.

ta**x**icab

The letter **x** can be at the

end of a word, like mailbox.

mailbo**x**

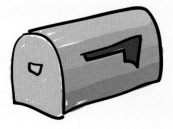

A box came in the mail. The box was

for **X**avier. It was sent from Texas. Why

would **X**avier get a box?

There was a note from Aunt Dixie. It

said that **X**avier should not open the

box until exactly nine o'clock. What

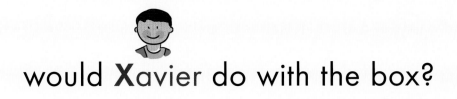

would **X**avier do with the box?

It was exactly two o'clock. Xavier had to

leave for the doctor. Today he had to go

for an **X** ray. **X**avier took the box with him.

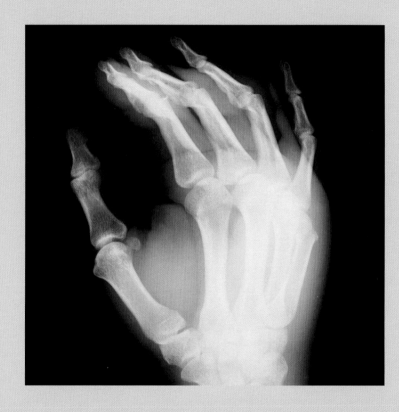

It was exactly four o'clock. 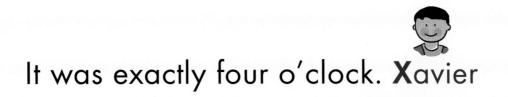**X**avier

exited the room after his **X** ray. There

was his friend, Max! Max had the

chicken pox. Poor Max.

Where was the box? **X**avier and Max ran

back into the **X**-ray room. Max found the

box and gave it to **X**avier. Extra-strong

tape kept the box sealed tight and safe!

It was exactly eight o'clock. **X**avier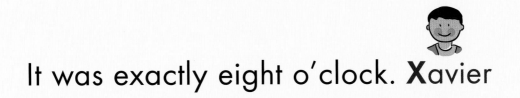

was extremely excited. He needed to

relax. When would it be exactly nine

o'clock?

It was exactly nine o'clock. **X**avier was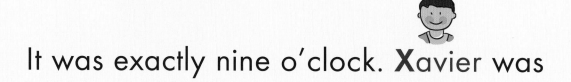

excited to see what was in the box. He

opened his box. What was in the box?

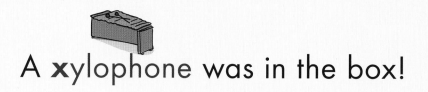

A **x**ylophone was in the box!

21

Fun Facts

Have you ever had an **X**-ray picture taken? **X** rays are a form of energy, like visual light. But **X** rays are invisible and can pass through solid objects. **X** rays are very important in medicine because, using **X** rays, doctors can photograph the inside of a person's body. **X** rays are often used to take pictures of teeth, bones, and organs. **X** rays are also used to treat cancer because they kill off cancer cells.

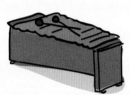

A **x**ylophone is a musical instrument. It is made up of many wooden bars arranged like the keys of a piano. The **x**ylophone is a percussion instrument, like the drum, and is played by hitting the bars with a mallet. (A mallet is like a hammer made out of plastic or rubber.) A **x**ylophone's bars are different lengths and give different sounds when struck. The word *xylophone* is a combination of two Greek words. *Xylon* means "wood," and *phone* means "sound." Therefore, *x*ylophone literally means "the sound of wood!"

To Read More

About the Letter X

Flanagan, Alice K. *A Fox: The Sound of X*. Chanhassen, Minn.: The Child's World, 2000.

About X rays

Gherman, Beverly, and Stephen Marchesi (illustrator). *The Mysterious Rays of Dr. Röntgen*. New York: Atheneum, 1994.

Zonta, Pat, and Clive Dobson (illustrator). *Jessica's X-Ray*. Toronto: Firefly Books, 2002.

About Xylophones

Poffenberger, Nancy. *Nursery Rhymes with Bells and Xylophone*. Cincinnati: The Fun Publishing Company, 1986.

Powell, Richard, and Simon Abel (illustrator). *Play along Farm*. New York: Simon & Schuster, 2001.

Words with X

Words with X at the Beginning

X ray

Xavier

X-ray

xylophone

Words with X in the Middle

dixie

exactly

excited

exited

extra-strong

extremely

taxicab

texas

Words with X at the End

box

mailbox

max

pox

relax

About the Authors

Cynthia Klingel has worked as a high school English teacher and an elementary teacher. She is currently the curriculum director for a Minnesota school district. Cynthia Klingel lives with her family in Mankato, Minnesota.

Robert B. Noyed started his career as a newspaper reporter. Since then, he has worked in communications and public relations for a Minnesota school district for more than fourteen years. Robert B. Noyed lives with his family in Brooklyn Center, Minnesota.